THE NEW AGE

TauroN
THE POUNDING
FURY

With special thanks to Troon Harrison

For all the Adams boys, older and younger

www.beastquest.co.uk

ORCHARD BOOKS
338 Euston Road, London NW1 3BH
Orchard Books Australia
Level 17/207 Kent St, Sydney, NSW 2000

A Paperback Original
First published in Great Britain in 2012

Beast Quest is a registered trademark of Beast Quest Limited
Series created by Beast Quest Limited, London

Text © Beast Quest Limited 2012
Inside illustrations by Pulsar Estudio (Beehive Illustration)
Cover by Steve Sims © Orchard Books 2012

A CIP catalogue record for this book is available from
the British Library.

ISBN 978 1 40831 846 1

1 3 5 7 9 10 8 6 4 2

Printed and bound by CPI Group (UK) Ltd, Croydon, CR0 4YY

Orchard Books is a division of Hachette Children's Books,
an Hachette UK company

www.hachette.co.uk

TAURON
THE POUNDING
FURY

BY ADAM BLADE

ORCHARD

I heard of Avantia in my youth, when
I flew with the other children over the
plains of Henkrall. They said it was a land
of beauty, bravery and honour. A place of
noble Beasts, too.

Even then it made me sick.

I can't fly now. My cruel mistress, Kensa,
was jealous of my wings, so she took them.
Don't pity me, Avantians – it's you who
should be afraid. Your time is coming.
Kensa has plans for your green and
pleasant land. Your Good Beasts will be
no defence against her servants – they'll
be powerless!

You'll need more than courage to protect
you from the Beasts of Henkrall!

Your sworn enemy,

Igor

PROLOGUE

Wind moaned across the vast plain, rustling the grass. Derma glanced around uneasily and tightened her grip on the reins. Her flying stallion, Sheza, flapped his black wings harder, battling the gusts. A restless energy filled the air and tingled on the back of Derma's neck. Below her on the ground, the buffalo herd snorted and pawed as if they too sensed the strange aura.

In her long life, Derma had survived many storms without fear. Even as a tiny child, she had been brave. Her father used to lift her onto the herd's gentlest buffalo. "It's too dangerous!" her mother would protest in shock, but Derma loved the woolly beasts. All she had to do was tickle the buffalo's ears to make it grow quiet. Her father seemed to pass on this gift without having to explain it to Derma. Soon she understood her destiny was to be a Buffalo Whisperer, just like him.

Although her life since then had been solitary, with only animals for company, Derma had endured it with courage. She had survived grass fires, blizzards, and tornadoes. She had nursed her herd through sickness and lean times. So why did she feel dread chilling her now? Derma noticed a smudge of dark clouds building over the distant mountains that ringed the plain. A storm was brewing, just as she'd suspected. *It might be best to keep the herd close to the barn tonight,* Derma thought.

She nudged her heels into Sheza and they flew in a circle above the herd. The buffalo bunched into a tight group. With a whistle, Derma commanded Sheza to the ground and he landed lightly in the waving grass. Derma guided him towards the barn, knowing that the buffalo would follow, eager for their evening grain. Although the shaggy creatures had stunted wings, they seldom used them. Trotting through the grass was easier for them than trying to keep their bulk airborne.

Sudden thunder shook the ground and Derma felt the vibrations in her chest. She glanced around in shock. No, it wasn't thunder— it was a stampede! A dark wave of buffalo poured towards her. Derma jerked Sheza's reins and the stallion jumped quickly aside. Bellowing, the buffalo rushed by, their eyes rolling in panic. Sheza flung his head up and shied sideways. *That was close!* Derma thought. *We were almost trampled.*

The herd did not slow down as it neared the homestead. It ran right through a fence, splintering the posts and shattering the rails. Some buffalo charged into the barn, wrenching the door right off its hinges. Others ran past and out across the plains. *They've never done anything like this before! Something is very wrong – but what?*

Derma dug her heels into Sheza's flanks, and the stallion galloped over the plain in pursuit of the herd. She bent her head against the screaming wind. It was lucky that Sheza was such a strong, fast horse. With her own arthritic wings, Derma would not have been able to fly after the herd herself.

Something like lightning slashed past Sheza's neck. The stallion skidded to a halt with a wild neigh. The tough leather reins dangled limp from Derma's hands. Each one had been sliced clean through! Derma raised her head from Sheza's mane. A cry of terror broke from her lips.

Two massive buffalo hooves were planted in the grass. Raising her gaze, Derma saw a thick pelt of tattered fur, which filled her nose with a musky stink. The creature's upper half was a human body, its wide chest knotted with muscle. Strong arms held a gleaming two-pronged sword.

It must have been the sword that cut through Sheza's reins.

Derma whimpered as the buffalo-man

stared down at her. His broad face was pulled into a grotesque grimace and his eyes glowed an unnatural, sickly yellow. Giant twisting horns sprouted from either side of his head. They pointed towards Derma as he lowered his head menacingly. His hind feet pawed the ground, sending up a spray of dirt.

He slashed his two-pronged sword through the air again. Its blades narrowly missed Sheza's shoulder as the horse shied backwards. Derma cried out, slipping half out of her saddle, then she fell.

Derma hit the ground hard, pain exploding across her back. Rolling over, she covered her face with one hand. Through her fingers, she glimpsed her attacker's contorted face looming above her. The points of his horns jabbed closer as the creature

bent his head. His grimace relaxed into a leering grin. *He knows I'm helpless now*, Derma thought as she lay sprawled in the grass. The drum beat of hooves filled her ears as Sheza galloped away. In the distance, her herd lowed in distress and scattered.

This is my final end, Derma thought. *Even my animals have abandoned me…*

CHAPTER ONE

THE FINAL TEST

Tom pulled the collar of his tunic tighter as the rain splashed down. His flying horse, Tempest, struggled against the buffeting wind as they soared above the land of Henkrall.

"We're in for a storm!" Elenna shouted.

She crouched over the ruff of her black wolf, Spark. Like Tempest, Spark strained to beat his wings

against the gusts. Tom still missed
Storm and Silver, their faithful
animals left behind in Avantia,
but he was grateful for their new
companions. Tempest and Spark
had proven their loyalty many
times on their Quest in Henkrall.

Rain pelted Tom harder, stinging
his face. The purple fur on Tempest's
shoulders and neck was matted
with water already. Tom's hands
were chilled and his knuckles were
a mottled blue. He watched as the
gloomy clouds sank lower, swirling
around them in every direction.
They had left behind the northern
forests and now curtains of mist
blanketed the dark peaks and slopes
of mountain ranges.

"I wish we could land!" Tom called
to Elenna. "I need to check the map!"

"So do I – but where?" replied his friend. "This kingdom is so hilly."

The rain thickened, and seemed to fall in a solid sheet. It poured over Tom, heavy as a waterfall. He squinted his eyes almost shut, and lowered his face to his chest. Far beneath, the forests of Henkrall's mountains lurched past. Ridge after ridge faded into the pouring rain like waves in a great ocean.

Tom glanced uneasily at Tempest's wide wings. Could their animals fly much longer in such conditions? Tom patted the horse in encouragement.

Elenna gasped, pointing. Tom squinted through the sheets of rain to see what she had spotted. Just over the next mountain range, a flat plain stretched ahead. It was so vast that the mountains ringing it were tiny

in the far distance. The grass covering
the plain glowed a brilliant green.

"It's perfect for us!" Tom said.

As they soared over the final peaks,
Tom nudged Tempest downwards.
The stallion swooped in wide arcs,
dropping toward the plain. Despite the
cold, pounding rain, and the roaring
wind that filled his ears, Tom grinned.

This place is like the Avantian plain

where my good friend Tagus roams!

A wave of homesickness swept through Tom but he tried to ignore it. He and Elenna still had work to do here in Henkrall. He had to stay focused on their Quest against the evil witch, Kensa. She had stolen blood from the good Beasts of Avantia and mixed it with the earth of Henkrall. From this mixture she had shaped six figurines of new Beasts that were running amok in this kingdom. The witch had hoped to send her creations to Avantia, but now only one remained. *But even one will be enough to kill hundreds of innocent people*, thought Tom.

He looked across at Elenna. Her dark hair was plastered to her head, and her tunic was soaked through. She steered Spark closer to Tempest so that the tips of their wings almost touched.

"I'm worried about this storm," Tom shouted. "If there's lightning, Kensa will try to transport the last Beast along the Lightning Path and into Avantia."

"I'd love to go straight to Kensa's palace and tackle her!" Elenna yelled.

"If we defeat Tauron first," Tom replied, "then Kensa's plan will be ruined anyway."

He saw Elenna shivering. He was chilled and hungry too. *I wonder if my father, Taladon, was ever this weary and weak on his Quests*, he thought.

Tom felt a frown of grief tighten his face. Taladon's body lay in Avantia's Gallery of Tombs, and the brave knight would never face another battle. *My suffering isn't important,*

Tom realized. *All that matters is living up to my father's legend. Aduro must have believed I could do this. Or, at least, he hoped I could.*

The old wizard had staked his own reputation by sending Tom and Elenna to Henkrall along the Lightning Path. Now King Hugo and all Avantians were relying on him and Elenna to complete this Quest successfully, preventing Kensa's evil from ever reaching their beautiful kingdom.

Turning his thoughts away from his homeland, Tom stared downwards as the grassy plain swept closer. Perhaps he would find Tauron and battle him very soon. Tom flexed his stiff leg and arm muscles, preparing for the fight that surely lay ahead.

CHAPTER TWO

ALONE IN THE STORM

Tempest lurched lower, pawing at the wind-blasted grass. With a jolt that jarred Tom's bones, his hooves hit the ground and the stallion cantered to a halt. Once Tom dismounted, the horse folded his dripping wings. Tom watched to make sure that Spark and Elenna landed safely too.

"Where are we?" his friend called over.

Tom pulled the shield from his back and checked the map scored on its wooden surface. It was getting harder to read the map as the shield refilled with magical tokens. They had been gifts from the Good Beasts of Avantia and each one gave Tom a special power. When he and Elenna first arrived in Henkrall, the six tokens had disappeared. Not a great way to start the Quest! But with each victory over one of Henkrall's Beasts, a token had returned to his shield. Now only the horseshoe of Tagus was missing.

Tom wiped rain from the shield with one hand and traced a route over the mountains until he came to the plain's open space. The name *Tauron* was written across it.

"It looks like we're in the right place," he muttered.

"You mean the Beast is here somewhere?" asked Elenna, scanning the plain.

Tom nodded. *But what should we be looking for?* he thought. *What kind of monstrous being has Kensa created with the blood of Tagus? Some kind of horse monster to gallop over the plains?* Tom strained his ears, listening for hoofbeats.

"Come on, show yourself!" he muttered.

He ran his hands over the recovered tokens. He felt sure he would need their powers before this Quest was completed. Then he turned to tell Elenna what he had learned from the map. She and Spark were standing some paces away, and she was staring hard across the windswept plain, her tunic billowing.

"What can you see?" he asked.

"I'm not sure..." she replied.

Tom focused on the power of the Golden Helmet. Though it was safe in the armoury at King Hugo's castle, it gave him powerful vision.

There – what was that slumped in the grass? Tom's hand dropped to the hilt of his sword.

A gust lifted away a curtain of rain and Tom saw more clearly. "It's a person!" he said.

Spark ran towards the figure, whining anxiously. Tom and Elenna sprinted after the wolf, splashing through deep puddles. Wet grass slapped Tom's thighs. Twice he slipped on the muddy ground and almost fell. Even Tempest stumbled as he trotted after Tom. The storm was changing the plain into a mud bath. Tom scanned the sky as he ran, dreading to see a fork of brilliant lightning slash open the dark clouds.

We don't have time for this distraction, Tom thought. *And what if it's a trap?* He slowed his pace as he approached the body, and gripped his sword hilt tighter. Crouching down, Tom saw an elderly woman with braided grey hair. Around her the grass was trampled, and the ground was gouged with deep marks. Spark sniffed at them suspiciously, growling.

"Is she alive?" Tom asked.

Elenna laid a hand on the woman's shoulder. Her eyelids fluttered. She writhed weakly as though trying to escape. "Help...help me!" she muttered.

"We won't hurt you," Elenna

reassured her. She turned to Tom.
"Let's get her off the wet ground."

Tom gently took one arm under
the shoulder and raised the woman
as Elenna helped. The old woman's
eyes flared wide with panic. They
focused on Elenna and the ghost of a
smile replaced the fearful expression.
Reaching with a muddy hand, the
woman stroked Elenna's cheek.

"I recognize a kindred spirit," she

croaked. "You have the power of healing, don't you girl?"

When Elenna's cheeks became rosy, Tom started in surprise. He couldn't remember seeing Elenna blush before!

"My grandmother taught me the use of herbs," Elenna replied, sounding shy. "But I wouldn't call that a healing power."

"I'm never wrong about these things," the old woman said. "I was born with it and have had it all my life."

"Who are you?" Elenna asked.

"I'm Derma," said the woman. "Tell me girl, are you good with animals too?"

Tom sighed. They didn't really have time for this conversation, even if it was pleasant. Had Elenna forgotten the danger to Henkrall? And what about the threat to Avantia? The Quest must be their focus!

But, said a voice in the back of his mind, *when we come across stranded people, a Beast is often involved!*

"What are you doing out here, alone on the plain?" Tom asked.

"I've lived here all my years," said Derma. "I was rounding up my herd of buffalo, but…but I fell off my horse."

From the fear that still played across her face, Tom sensed she was lying. Or at least not telling the full truth.

"You must know this landscape very well if you ride on it, and fly over it," Tom said. "Perhaps you could help us to track something."

Elenna shot Tom an irritated scowl.

"She's too weak to help us," she whispered. She laid a comforting arm around the old woman's shoulders. "Don't worry about tracking anything," she said. "Where do you live? We'll take you home."

Derma pointed a frail finger off to the west, and Tom saw a huddled homestead with a cabin and barns.

"Great!" Elenna said. "Perhaps we can all dry off and even share a meal with you." She stared directly at Tom as she spoke.

She's trying to tell me to calm down, he realised. *And she's right, we do need to rest. But how can we? The fate of two kingdoms is at stake!*

Tom realised he was bunching his hands into fists. He forced himself to relax and tried to smile at Derma. It felt more like a tight grimace of impatience, but it was the best he could manage.

"Come on then," he said. "Let's get you home." He took one of the woman's arms and hurried her through the soaking grass. As they hustled along, with the animals following, Tom scanned in every direction.

If it was the Beast that had frightened Derma, where is it now?

CHAPTER THREE

SHAME

Trudging through the storm, Tom searched for clues. What kind of Beast would be out here on this wind-blasted expanse? There was so little shelter in any direction. And why was this woman, Derma, out here so far from any village? She'd said she was herding buffalo but Tom hadn't seen any. What were these powers she spoke of? Suddenly, a terrible thought occurred to him. *What if she's a witch? Another minion of Kensa's sent to ambush us...*

"Why were you herding on your own?" Tom asked. He didn't risk looking at Elenna. He was sure she'd be glaring at him.

"But see, I wasn't alone," Derma replied as they trudged on. "I was with my stallion, Sheza. There was a strange feeling in the air – it gave me chills. Then the herd spooked – I've never seen the like before! They nearly ran me down. I knew something was very wrong..."

Her eyes became glassy and she faltered as a strong wind whipped past. Tom waited for a lull in the gale.

"Did something attack you?" he asked.

"It can't have been real..." Derma muttered.

"Tell us," said Tom, more fiercely than he intended. Elenna shot him an angry look.

Derma swallowed. "It was a terrifying thing," she said. "I was so frightened my teeth rattled. Some sort of creature. A buffalo-man, huge, ugly, and stinking. He had horns and a forked sword that cut—"

"I knew it!" Tom interrupted. "It's Tauron, our next Beast!"

He felt Derma cower in his grip. She stumbled as tears welled in her eyes. *She's no witch*, Tom thought. *Just a frightened old woman.*

But there wasn't time to worry about her now. He quickened his stride. Derma's homestead lay just ahead, a shadow in the driving rain. Soon the log walls of barns and the cabin rose around them. Buffalo lowed inside one barn and Tom glimpsed their woolly shapes as he strode by.

"There's grain in there for your horse," Derma said, sounding at the end of her strength.

"Tempest and Spark!" Elenna called over her shoulder. "Shelter in the barn!" The animals seemed to understand and trotted inside.

Rain poured from the thatched cabin roof. Tom flung open the front door and the three of them tumbled in, then Elenna banged the door shut and bolted it. The noise of the wind sank to a dull moan. Warmth flowed from an open fire in the room beyond. Derma went slack with exhaustion in Tom's grip, and he lowered her into a chair.

"I have a pot of soup in the other

room," she said. "It might still be warm.

Elenna pulled Tom into the second room, then rounded on him, her eyes blazing. "Remind me why you're doing this Quest exactly?" she demanded. "For the good of Henkrall and Avantia? Or for your

own personal glory? You wouldn't want to fail because you were helping a stranded traveller who happens to live in Henkrall, would you, Tom? Where would be the glory in that?"

Tom's heart tightened at her sarcastic tone. "I'm only trying to live up to my father's memories."

Elenna snorted. "Your father! I'm sure Taladon would be proud to see you bullying a frightened old woman with impatient questions!"

Elenna spun on her heel and stalked back into the room where Derma sat. Tom stayed rooted to the spot, feeling wet, cold, hungry, and filled with shame.

Elenna came back in, supporting the old woman. Tom went to the fire and placed a dry log in the embers.

"Help yourself to food," said Derma,

waving her hand at a black pot. Elenna carried it over to the fire and placed it on a tripod over the growing flames.

Soon she was ladling bowls of soup from the cauldron. Tom bent his face over his bowl. The rich broth of buffalo meat and roots tasted delicious, but Tom barely noticed. His thoughts were in turmoil.

Taladon, my father, was a hero because he faced each threat with courage. I only want to succeed in my Quests like he did! That's all I'm trying to do! But Taladon was always kind. And I haven't been kind today...

Wind rattled the windows and the fire fluttered. Their clothing steamed in the warmth. Tom's shame grew heavier in his chest until he could hardly breathe.

"I'm sorry," Tom whispered to his friend. "My father wouldn't be proud of my behaviour today. But can't you understand? I have to defeat this final Beast and then defeat Kensa... before it's too late! The storm is growing worse. What if we don't find the Beast in time, and Kensa uses lightning to send him to Avantia?"

Elenna paused, the spoon halfway to her mouth. Her face was pinched with fatigue. "You're right," she said. "So much is at stake, but we're both exhausted. We shouldn't use energy on arguing when we could work together, like we usually do."

"This soup will strengthen us," Tom said. "Then we can go and find Tauron. We know he's very close by."

Even as Tom spoke, thunder growled across the plain and echoed

44

against the mountains. Dread curdled in Tom's stomach. Where there was thunder, there was lightning.

CHAPTER FOUR

THE BLOOD OF TAGUS

Tom and Elenna gulped their soup, then headed for the cabin door.

Derma hobbled after them. "You young ones came along just in time. I was wet and shaky as a new born calf!"

"We're glad we could help," Tom said. As he reached for the door latch, Derma clutched his arm.

"Wait, young stranger. I must tell you one last thing about the creature that attacked me."

"What is it?" Tom asked.

"I have a sixth sense for animals. Behind its sword and horns, that creature has a heart that was once good."

Tom nodded and patted her hand. "Rest and don't worry, we'll take care of the Beast."

He swung the door open and stepped into the storm's fury with Elenna at his heels.

Derma is right, Tom thought as he ran towards the barn. *Each Beast has been created from the blood of a Good Beast. This time, Kensa must have used the blood of my old friend Tagus. I owe it to him to defeat Tauron.*

Reaching the barn, they found the

animals by a trough. The remaining buffalo were keeping a safe distance from Spark. Tom rubbed Tempest's neck. "Be brave once more," he said. "This is our last battle together, I hope." The horse's ears twitched and he flexed his mighty wings. Tom grabbed a handful of mane and jumped onto Tempest's back. Spark dropped a bone he was gnawing and greeted Elenna with a lick to her

cheek. For a moment, her face relaxed into a smile. Then it set into grim lines of determination, and she climbed onto the wolf's back and gripped his pelt.

"Let's find Tauron!" she said.

Outside, the animals fought to get airborne as vicious blasts hammered them. Finally they struggled aloft and managed to clear the barn roof. Tom clung fiercely to Tempest's mane. He strained his ears, listening for thunder, but the shriek of the wind and the roar of the downpour filled his head. He peered at the plain sliding beneath them. *It's impossible to see anything in this storm!*

The wind rose to a screaming howl, sucking the breath from Tom's lungs. His tunic was flung over his face. Tempest pitched sideways, neighing in alarm. Tom righted him, and saw Spark to his left, barely able to steady himself. The wolf spun in the violent currents and Elenna's hair was blown about in a wild tangle.

"This is hopeless," Tom shouted. "We'll have to land again!" He nudged Tempest down. Tempest's hooves hit with a thud and slipped sideways. The horse pitched to his knees. Tom slid over Tempest's shoulder into wind-flattened grass and thick, slimy mud. As they struggled to stand, Spark landed nearby with Elenna clinging on. The wolf's paws scrabbled to find a foothold.

"It's too slippery to risk riding. We'll have to walk!" Tom said.

The four of them staggered across the plain's vast expanse. "How can we possibly fight anything in these conditions?" Tom muttered.

"I can barely keep my balance long enough to string an arrow," Elenna said.

"It doesn't look like we're going to find the Beast anyway," Tom said in despair. "It's too hard to see out here."

Something brilliant and sharp flickered overhead.

Lightning? But I didn't hear any thunder! Tom's heart clenched. He stared intently into the swirling mist. Another glimmer. *That's not lightning...*

"Watch out!" he yelled to Elenna, jerking back. A two-pronged sword, its blade honed to a lethal edge, flashed ahead. Tom reached for his own sword and held its point high. He turned on the spot, trying to glimpse the invisible attacker. A great body loomed through the fog. Rain shone on the twisted horns that jutted above the Beast's face. From his human shoulders and buffalo legs hung a thick, shaggy coat. Rain had turned it into sodden ropes of hair. Tom gave a choking cough as its musky stench filled his throat.

"Tauron!" he breathed.

An arrow whizzed past as Elenna launched an attack. With amazing speed, the Beast snatched the arrow from the air. Tom had never seen reflexes so fast. Effortlessly, the Beast's human fist snapped the arrowhead from the shaft. He hurled the flint head back at Elenna, and she ducked as it missed by a hair's breadth.

The Beast turned and galloped away on his hind legs. His wide buffalo hooves, each the size of cartwheels, seemed to have no problem running in the gooey mud. In his hands, he held the forked sword aloft, slashing at tattered clouds.

"We mustn't let him escape!" Tom cried. He rushed forward, forgetting the slippery ground in his haste. With a wallop, he fell backwards, rain pelting his face. Stiff with cold, he climbed to his feet. His tunic was plastered in mud. Tempest trotted to him and stood with his head bent patiently.

"You're right," Tom said. "We going to have to take to the air to chase this Beast, no matter how dangerous." He mounted Tempest and the horse flapped his wings hard. "Stay here!" Tom called to Elenna. "Tempest's a stronger flier than Spark."

Elenna nodded, stringing another arrow to her bow. As they rose off the plain, Tom's angled the stallion's head into the wind.

He could hear Tauron's hooves thumping the ground, and soon found the Beast galloping wildly across the plain. And straight towards Derma's home.

I've got to stop him! Tom thought.

CHAPTER FIVE

A DEADLY JOUST

He steered Tempest over the Beast
and dropped his hand to the hilt
of his sword. But Tauron spotted
him and lashed out with his forked
blade. Tempest reared back, his legs
wheeling, and the deadly weapon
scythed past his flank. Tom patted
the stallion's flank as they flew out
of reach.

Tauron watched them in the sky,

swinging his sword back and forth, as if taunting them to come closer. Tom was pleased to see no sign of the giant Lightning Staff. Without it, the Beast was at least stuck in Henkrall. Tom nudged Tempest closer to the Beast. *If I could just come at him from one side*, he thought, *I might be able to slip beneath his blade and take a swing at him.*

Tom pushed down firmly on Tempest's neck and the horse responded by folding his wings and dropping sharply. He dodged alongside Tauron's shoulder and Tom leaned far out from the horse's back, gripping with his legs. With one hand he held onto Tempest's mane. With the other hand, he swiped at the Beast. Tauron leapt sideways, and brought up his forked blade. It met Tom's with a ring of steel and a spray

of sparks. Almost over-balanced by
the force of the blow, Tom hauled
himself more firmly onto Tempest's
back.

He feinted a blow towards Tauron's
head. The Beast didn't flinch, but

raised his other hand and swatted at
Tempest's wings as though the horse
was an insect. The force of the blow
sent Tom and his flying steed reeling.
He managed to steady them and
turned back to face his foe.

Tauron snorted and turned, then
put on a burst of speed that carried
him off across the plain. Elenna
arrived at Tom's side, gripping Spark's
water-logged fur.

"I couldn't just stand around and
watch," she said. "Is he giving up?"

"I doubt it," Tom replied. "I think
he's just getting started."

Kensa's Beasts had all shown
themselves willing to fight to the
death, driven by the evil magic in
their hearts. Sure enough, Tauron
skidded to a halt and turned with
sword raised high. His broad chest

rose and fell with heavy breaths and his hooves gouged up great clods of earth.

"It's like he wants to joust!" said Elenna.

Tom pointed his own sword at the Beast. "Then I will meet him."

He felt Elenna's uncertain gaze upon him. "Are you sure?" she called. "He'll be able to throw a lot more weight behind his blows."

A vision filled Tom's mind. The last battle of Taladon, his father, had been a joust. It had ended terribly as Taladon's blood stained the snow and his brave heart stopped beating.

"Don't try and stop me," he said. "He has the advantage of his bulk, but I can fly. I'd say it's an even match."

Elenna remained silent. *Who am I fooling?* thought Tom.

"Come on, boy," Tom urged, pressing his heels into Tempest's flanks. The horse's wings rose and fell in whooshing beats. As they flew towards Tauron, the Beast began to run at them, gaining speed with every stride. His polished buffalo hooves flashed almost silver and his bellowed challenge rose on the wind. Tom watched the double forked blades of Tauron's gleaming weapon, wondering how he could get past such a fearsome defence.

Then it came to him. *I don't have to get past it... Maybe I can make the Beast drop it!*

He grasped his sword hilt in both hands with all his strength, and hoped he could stay on Tempest with only the grip of his legs. As Tempest and Tauron surged towards each other,

Tom lifted his sword and waited for the
Beast to strike. As soon as his enemy's
sword sliced upwards, Tom aimed his
own into the space between Tauron's
twin blades. As the metal clashed, Tom
twisted his sword sideways. Tauron
roared in pain as his shoulder swivelled
back, but he didn't drop his sword as
Tom had hoped. He wheeled around
for another strike when a gust of wind

blew Tempest sideways. Tom lost his grip and fell from the horse's back. He pitched past the Beast's hairy legs and, thinking fast, he jack-knifed in the air, his arms flung out. He grabbed at the Beast's sodden leg hair, stopping his headlong fall.

"Go!" he called to Tempest. "Fly to safety."

The stallion hesitated for a moment, then broke away as Tauron raised his sword. Somehow, Tom realised, the Beast hadn't even noticed he was nestled in the thick hair on his upper leg.

And that gives me a few precious moments, Tom thought.

Clinging to the Beast's fur with one hand, Tom sheathed his sword and reached for the ruby at his waist. The bright red jewel, won from Torgor the Minotaur, allowed him to communicate with Beasts. Tauron might be stronger and faster, but Tom had knowledge that the Beast lacked.

I just hope this works, he thought.

CHAPTER SIX

A MESSAGE TO THE BEAST

Clutching the jewel tightly, Tom squeezed his eyes shut. He tried to ignore the Beast's bellows of rage and his own fear of being trampled. He hung onto the stinking hair and concentrated on the message in his mind.

Kensa doesn't care about you. She's just using you for her own evil purposes.

Was Tauron listening? Tom didn't

know, but at least the Beast was standing still, the sword raised in a motionless arm. Tom kept sending his message.

Kensa has everything she needs. She is just using you to distract me.

Tom knew his message wasn't quite true. Kensa needed Tauron to travel the Lightning Path to Avantia. She was desperate for her last Beast to wreak havoc there. Hastily, Tom pushed this thought from his mind. He had to convince Tauron that he was useless to his mistress.

Tom saw the Beast had spotted him. His yellow eyes dimmed. Tauron lowered his sword. *Perhaps I'm getting through*, thought Tom.

Kensa made you, and she'll get rid of you just as easily.

Tauron's staring eyes flared in

sudden anger, and he swiped at Tom with one hand. Tom tried to dodge, but there was nowhere to go. Tauron gripped him by a leg, pulled him free, and hoisted him high into the air.

The Beast dangled Tom in front of his horned face. As Tom hung suspended, he saw Elenna in the corner of his eye. She was hovering on Spark, lining up an arrow towards

the Beast's head.

"No!" Tom shouted. "I'm getting through to him!"

Tauron's mouth opened to reveal blackened teeth. The Beast started to lower Tom towards them. Tom held his nerve.

Kensa has the staff and the jewel, he tried. *She doesn't need you.*

The Beast moaned in distress and his grip on Tom weakened.

I'm not your enemy, Tom said with his mind.

Tauron began to lower him, but when Tom was level with his chest, the Beast froze. His head tilted as though listening to something and he shifted on his hooves.

"Faithful Beast, help is here!" shouted a voice overhead.

"Igor!" shouted Elenna.

Oh no! Tom slotted the ruby into his shield and drew his sword. With a swipe, he rapped the Beast's knuckles with the flat side of the blade. Tauron released him with a roar. Tom turned over in the air and thumped to the ground, ankle-deep in mud.

Tom scanned the sky and saw Igor circling above on his winged hog. Ropes hung from a harness

attached to the hog's body. Tom's heart pounded when he saw what was suspended beneath. A metal rod almost three times as tall as Tom.

The Lightning Staff!

Tom hadn't seen the Staff since Igor stole it from the village of Herrinfell, and now it had the Jewel of Journeys set into its head. One bolt of lightning and the Staff's carrier would be transported to Avantia!

An arrow whizzed past Tom's head and he ducked. For a moment he thought Elenna was aiming at him, but then another shot by. Each one lodged in the thick hair around the Beast's hoof. Another hit the mark with pinpoint accuracy. *She's pinning him down!* Tom realised.

Elenna loosed a volley of arrows. Each one snagged a lock of hair from around Tauron's hooves and sank into the ground.

"Tauron, your mistress counts on your success!" Igor yelled. "Soon you'll gallop through the green fields of Avantia. I hear it is a fair land. Isn't that right, Tom? But Avantia won't be fair for much longer!" He loosened the harness and the Staff fell through the air.

Tauron bellowed in triumph and reached up. He snatched the Staff and held it aloft. Thunder roared and dark clouds piled up, churning like a witch's brew. At any moment, lightning would crackle across the sky. And then…

Tom shuddered at the thought. *I won't let this foul Beast find a way to Avantia!*

There was only one hope left – Tom had to reach Tauron's heart. He knew it held the key to the Beast's strength.

He scrambled to his feet and began to haul himself up on strands of hair. Tauron seemed too busy watching the sky to notice. Lightning flashed in a sheet overhead.

"Watch out for the boy!" cried Igor.

Tauron gave a snort of alarm as he noticed Tom. He staggered and turned his sword point on Tom.

"Look out, Tom!" yelled Elenna.

As Tauron stabbed, Tom let go of the Beast's fur with one hand and swung himself sideways. The blade swiped past, just missing him, and plunged into the Beast's own chest. Tauron gave a strangled, ear-splitting shriek and fell to his knees.

"No!" Igor wailed.

In moments, the ropes of hair in Tom's hands dissolved into the rain. The Beast's great body was shrinking.

Tom leapt away as far as he could, rolling in the muddy plain.

When he looked up, he thought a tree was falling towards him. But then he realised it was the Lightning Staff, dropping from the Beast's limp hand. Tom could do nothing as the metal rod toppled towards him.

CHAPTER SEVEN

KENSA'S REVENGE

A hand hooked under Tom's shoulder and heaved him clear. As the Staff slammed into the marshy ground, it coated him with a spray of mud. He saw Elenna leaning from Spark's back, a grin on her face. She must have swooped past just in time.

"Thanks!" said Tom.

He stared in shock at Tauron's body – a steaming pile of mud mixed with a

few clumps of fur. It was the last anyone would see of a Beast that should never have existed. Tom dragged his feet through the mud and found Tagus's horseshoe, all that remained of Tauron's heart. He slotted it beside the other five tokens in his shield.

"Tom! Look!" Elenna shouted, pointing to the sky. Tom raised his face and realised the rain had stopped falling. He understood why his friend sounded alarmed. The dark clouds, filled with flashing lightning, were rolling north.

Towards Kensa's palace!

Igor swooped past, his face lit up in a wicked grin. "It's not over, heroes of Avantia."

"Kensa hasn't given up yet!" Tom said. "She has a Lightning Staff of her own!"

"We need to defeat her face to face," Elenna said. "Let's fly!"

Tom called to Tempest and the stallion landed beside him. He mounted, feeling desperation cloud any hope in his heart. How much longer could they keep going? The brave stallion struggled into the air alongside Spark.

"Just one more fight, boy," Tom encouraged his horse. "Then you can rest in a warm stable."

Mountain ranges sped by below, half-buried in mist. Rocks stuck up like fangs. They overtook the storm clouds, which still drifted north.

Tom used the power of the Golden Helmet to look ahead and see Igor streaking towards Kensa's lair. The hog's wings were a blur.

"He's getting away!" said Elenna.

"Igor's not our problem anymore," said Tom. "If Kensa returns to Avantia on the Lightning Path, we'll be stuck here unable to help."

Tom scanned the horizon and finally saw Kensa's palace perched on a jutting peak.

"We can't just fly there without a plan!" Elenna called.

Tom knew they didn't have much time, but his friend was right. "Let's find a clearing to land," said Tom.

"Over there!" Tom pointed to an open meadow at the base of Kensa's mountain lair. As they guided the animals down, Tom saw ramshackle wooden huts beneath some trees on one side of the field.

"Who do you think lives there?" Elenna asked as Spark and Tempest landed nearby.

"I don't know," Tom replied, drawing his sword, "but we should be careful."

Followed by the animals, they trudged across the rough ground. The witch's castle towered to one side, piercing the low cloud with its steep tiled roofs. Strange pale light flickered in its narrow windows.

The door of a hut opened and a group of men and women ran out to meet them. At their head strode Old Peter, the trader who'd sold them Tempest and Spark when they first arrived in Henkrall. Tom sheathed his sword and stood open-mouthed. "What are you doing here?"

"Don't you remember?" asked Peter. "I said I would come to investigate what Kensa was up to." He indicated the rest of the men and woman. "We picked up some more rebels on the way."

Hope brought fresh strength to

Tom and he hurried to meet the men. *Old Peter has helped us before. Perhaps now he has information that will help us make a plan.*

"Kensa's last Beast is destroyed," he said. "Tell me what you've discovered about the witch's workshop."

The rebels of Henkrall scowled grimly. "We've discovered nothing,

and we're not trying again,"
the trader warned. "Look what
happened!" He pulled another man
forward. His face was covered with
cuts and one eye was swollen shut
with a bruise.

"What happened?" Elenna asked.

"We sent him to spy on the
workshop. But he was ambushed by
a flightless man with a chain whip.
Lucky to escape with his life, he was."

"Igor," Tom said. "He'll be telling
Kensa that her Beasts are all
defeated."

"And she'll be waiting for us,"
Elenna added.

"We should leave the animals
behind," said Tom. "If we lose, Kensa
will take no prisoners. And if we win,
we'll soon be back in Avantia and
have no need of them."

Elenna looked sad as she bent down to Spark. "You're as brave as my wolf Silver," she said. "I wish you could meet and run together in the moonlight."

Tom laid a hand on Tempest's neck. "You're a fine horse and have served me well," he said. "I'll miss you."

Tempest tossed his head, eyes glowing. It seemed to Tom that it was a glow of pride.

Tom turned to the waiting trader. "Will you take these animals and make sure they are well treated?" he asked.

Old Peter frowned. "I'll find them good homes," he replied. "But I'm afraid I can't return your money."

"This isn't about money," Tom said. "It's about your freedom – and our lives."

CHAPTER EIGHT

THE WITCH'S WORKSHOP

Tom and Elenna stared at the sharp
spires of the castle. Rain shone on its
walls of stone. Thunder rolled nearby
– soon the lightning would come.

"It's now or never," Tom said,
drawing up his courage.

"But how can we get in?" Elenna
asked. "We can't just walk in the
front door."

Tom studied the walls. He couldn't even see a front door! The workshop was in a tower on the southern corner. Thick ropes of ivy smothered the wall and coiled around the narrow arched windows.

"We'll climb up there," Tom said.

They darted across the meadow to the slippery rocks piled at the base of the tower.

Tom placed a foot on the first rock and gripped a crack with his fingers. Then he sprang upwards, caught hold of the next slab, and heaved himself over it. Soon he was panting, and his hands were scratched and bleeding from the rocks' sharp edges. Elenna followed her own route up nearby.

They reached the tower wall. He turned to help Elenna up the last rock. Her breath was coming hard too, but there was no time to rest. They grabbed the ivy and began to climb higher. Tom tried not to look down. If he fell, Arcta's feather might save him. Elenna would not be so lucky. "Be careful where you put each foot," he said.

Reaching the windowsill, Tom raised his head cautiously over its edge. Luckily, Kensa had her back to the window. She wore her dark robe covered in strange symbols – cog-wheels, spindles, arrows and stars. Tom burned with desire to leap into the room then and there. But he had to be careful. Kensa was a powerful sorceress and he didn't know what secret weapons she might have ready. He noticed the window was slightly ajar and he pushed it further open.

It gave a tiny squeak, but Kensa didn't turn around.

She was peering into a cauldron of bubbling liquid that hung over a fire. All around her were jars of dark liquids, powders, and parts of long-dead creatures. Chunks of rocks and minerals lay scattered amongst the jars. In the shadows lurked mechanical devices with metal shafts and cogs. Tom remembered seeing them on his previous visit. Then everything had been neatly arranged. Now the workshop was in a mess, as though Kensa had been working feverishly. Tom studied the muddle, trying to devise a plan of attack.

I wish I understood all her powers, he thought. *At least she hadn't seen them yet. We can use surprise to our advantage.*

Kensa's red hair swung as she

walked to a shelf. Along it stood
the figurines of the Beasts she had
created from Henkrall's earth. Tom
scanned them with grim satisfaction.
He and Elenna had fought and
defeated every one.

"Useless, pathetic creatures!" Kensa
muttered, her lips curling. Igor
cowered at her side, smoothing her
robes as if to calm her down. Kensa
snatched the figurine of Tauron from

the shelf. Turning, she flung the Beast to shatter on the black tiled floor. Tom tensed.

"If I can't transport my Beasts to Avantia, I'll go there myself and make them pay!" Kensa's eyes blazed with fury. Igor snatched his hand from her robe and grovelled at her feet.

"And I know someone who might be able to help me," the witch muttered. Her face lit up with a sly smile.

"Me, mistress?" Igor whimpered. "Can I help you?"

"Useless idiot," Kensa snarled. Her kick to Igor's ribs sent the hunchback sprawling. His chain whip flew from his hand, skittering across the floor. "There's no way I'm taking you to Avantia with me," Kensa said.

She flung another Beast figurine – Flaymar this time – narrowly missing her minion.

Tears welled in Igor's eyes and pooled in the creases of his cheeks.

"She has to be stopped!" Tom whispered to Elenna. The thought of Kensa reaching Avantia was horrifying. *And who is this other person she's talking about?*

A cramp tightened in one of Tom's feet. He shifted it, trying to find firmer footing. A gasp from Elenna made him straighten and peer back through the window.

Igor was staring straight at them.

CHAPTER NINE

VANISHING ACT

"Mistress, beware!" Igor shrieked.
He scrambled to coil his chain whip.
With a quick twirl, he snapped
it towards Tom and Elenna. Tom
ducked as the glass of the window
shattered above his head. When he
looked in again past the jagged pane,
Kensa gave a cry of fury. She rushed
to a set of shelves and snatched up
her Lightning Staff. Tom hadn't

seen it there before.

"You can't win!" she snapped. "It's over, Tom!"

With her robes swirling, she raced towards the curve of a spiral stone stairway.

"Stand and fight!" Tom yelled.

"Keep them busy, Igor!" Kensa shrieked. She disappeared around the curve of the stairs.

"We have to stop her!" Elenna yelled. Tom pulled himself up and swung a leg over the windowsill. The hunchback swung another blow towards Tom, but he turned so it landed across his shield with a crack. Twisting at the waist, Tom reached out of the window.

"Grab my hand!" he called to Elenna. She climbed onto the window ledge and leapt down.

Igor jumped on a table, scattering glass vials onto the floor.

"I'll give you two a lashing!" he shouted. The chain landed across the shield again, almost driving Tom to his knees. He advanced slowly, sword drawn. Igor lunged from the table and battered the whip's heavy handle across the shield's face. Tom staggered, knocking Elenna into a table. Jars, potions, and strange metal tools clattered over. Tom dragged a shaken Elenna behind a set of shelves. "Follow my lead!" he whispered to his friend.

"You can't hide from Igor," snarled the hunchback.

As he raised his arm again, Tom shouldered into the shelves and Elenna lent her weight too. Igor screamed and pounced back as the shelves toppled, but they trapped his whip beneath. He fought to free it, yanking with all his strength.

Elenna leapt out, crouched, and swung her bow in a low arc, catching it against Igor's legs. He tumbled onto his backside with a cry.

"Curse you, Avantian scum!" he shouted.

"Leave him!" Tom shouted, jumping

over the remains of the Beast figures and heading for the stairs. "We've got to stop Kensa from reaching the roof!"

Tom pounded upward, slipping on the smooth stone. Elenna pressed behind him with her bow in one hand. They burst out of an arched door at the top of the stairs. Wind and rain whipped their faces. At the wall edging the turret roof, Kensa stood tall and rigid. Her robes flapped in the storm so that she looked like a giant bird of prey. She held the staff up to the rolling clouds. Thunder boomed and crashed so loudly that tiles vibrated beneath Tom's feet.

Far below, Tom saw the huddle of huts. The trader and his friends stood in the meadow, looking up at them.

A brilliant fork of lightning tore

open the sky. Tom felt the hair
on the back of his neck stand up.
The smell of sulphur burned his
nostrils.

"You thought you were so clever
defeating my Beasts," the witch
mocked them. "But you weren't
clever enough. Maybe you're too
young to be Master of the Beasts.
Now Aduro will see for himself
how you've failed!"

"You leave Aduro out of this!"
Tom shouted.

The witch gave a twisted smile.
She lifted her staff higher and began
to chant:

"Take me to Avantia,
There to break the King."

Tom roared in defiance. "You will
never reach Avantia," he cried, "not
while there's blood in my veins!"
He rushed across the rooftop and
snatched at a corner of the witch's
flapping cloak. Elenna jumped
forward beside Tom and gripped the
billowing fabric. Just as they grabbed
hold, lightning lit up the sky. Tom
squeezed closed his eyes, but the fork
of white light seemed to burn right
through his eyelids.

Tremendous fizzing energy ripped through Tom's body. His muscles twisted in rigid spasms of pain. He held on desperately as the witch rose with the hideous magic of the Lightning Path. She soared upwards, twirling and cackling and battered by wind.

"Don't let go!" Tom bellowed to Elenna.

Chaotic, dazzling lightning shredded the sky. When Kensa's staff pierced the clouds, she rose into their dark mist with Tom and Elenna still hanging on. The sky thundered, drowning out the witch's shrieks. Tom wondered if she was in pain or whether she was celebrating her success. He twisted his grip deeper into her cloak. Elenna clung beside him, her face tight with fear. If they

tumbled now, no magic would save
them. Helplessly, they were flung
through Henkrall's wild skies.

Another bolt of lightning flashed
and Tom's vision filled with searing
white light. He felt himself falling.

Has the Lightning Path failed? he
wondered. *Are we going to die?*

In a jumble of limbs, he landed
on hard ground. His head spun. He

opened his eyes slowly and realised he was seeing not lightning, but sunshine. Rain no longer soaked his face. Birdsong filled his ears and the smell of ripening fruit drifted into his nose. He heard Elenna groan. As his vision cleared, he saw gateposts and slowly realised where he was.

"King Hugo's Palace!" he gasped.

He was still holding Kensa's robe. Leaping to his feet, he pulled out his sword. As Kensa stood up, he levelled the tip of the blade at her throat. "Don't move," he warned her. The witch obeyed, but there seemed to be a glint of mocking amusement in her eyes. She held her staff loosely in one hand.

"That was rather fun, wasn't it?" she said.

Elenna managed to clamber up and

quickly notched an arrow to her bow.

"It won't be fun where you're going," she said. "There's a cold cell in the palace dungeon waiting for you. Right next door to Sanpao the Pirate King."

"You two deserve each other," Tom added.

To Tom's unease, the witch threw her head back and her red hair seemed to sparkle. Her eyes gleamed with delight. "The dungeons with Sanpao will suit me fine," she said.

Her body rippled then turned transparent. Tom staggered back in surprise. In less than heartbeat, she vanished. The tip of his sword wavered, pointing at nothing.

"Come on!" he said. "We have to warn King Hugo and Aduro!"

CHAPTER TEN

BLEAK FUTURE

Tom and Elenna ran through
the open gate and into the castle
courtyard.

"What's the rush?" asked Captain
Harkman, stepping from the
gatehouse.

"No time to explain!" Tom yelled
as they pounded across the sunlit
cobbles. They headed for the staircase
leading to the throne room. Before

they reached it, a loud explosion sent
clouds of smoke billowing upwards.
Tom skidded to a stop and saw a
commotion near the entrance to the
dungeons. A knot of guards surged
to and fro, struggling to hold back –
who? Tom squinted into the smoke.
Kensa swung her staff in a wide
arc, keeping the soldiers at bay. And
beside her ran Sanpao!

Tom rushed to help the guards but an excited dog dashed between his feet. He sprawled on the cobblestones. As he struggled up again, a shadow darkened the courtyard. The curved wooden hull of the pirate's flying ship soared overhead, all sails spread.

"Hove to, my hearties!" roared Sanpao. Two ropes unfurled over the ship's rail, their ends dangled in mid-air like writhing snakes.

"Block their escape!" shouted Tom. Elenna strung an arrow and fired at the ship. One shaft after another lodged in the hull, but none managed to cut the ropes.

"You scurvy wench!" a cowering pirate shouted, shaking his fist.

Captain Harkman slashed his sword towards Sanpao but the pirate was too fast. He snatched at a rope and twirled it, wrapping it around the captain's sword blade. Then he wrenched the blade from Harkman's hand. Tom joined the ring of guards and threw himself at Kensa. The witch's staff smashed down on Tom's blade and sent it spinning to the ground. She twirled in a circle, shooting brilliant sparks from her staff's head. Wide-eyed with fear, the guards jumped back. As Tom stooped to retrieve his sword, Kensa and Sanpao wriggled up the ropes towards the outstretched arms of the crew.

"Move your blubbery behind, Kensa!" ordered Sanpao with a laugh.

"Ha! I've seen weeds grow faster than you can climb!" the witch cackled.

"I've run out of arrows!" Elenna cried, arriving at Tom's side.

"They've not escaped yet!" said
Tom, as Sanpao and Kensa clambered
over the ship's rail. He ran towards

a nearby haycart, leapt onto the
back then threw himself into the air.
He managed to catch the end of a
dangling rope.

"Oh no, you don't!" roared Sanpao.
As he swung and climbed at the same
time, Tom saw the Pirate King leaning
over the rail with his cutlass drawn.
With a swipe of the blade, he severed
the rope and Tom plummeted back
into the hay.

"Unreef the main! Unfurl the topsails!" roared Sanpao. "All hands on deck!"

Tom heard pounding feet on the ship's timbers. Sails flapped open and filled with wind. With a creak of timbers, the mighty ship soared over the castle battlements.

"Nice travelling with you!" Kensa shouted mockingly to Tom and Elenna. "We should do it again sometime!" Her cackle of laughter was snatched by the wind as the ship grew rapidly smaller.

Tom climbed down with a heavy heart. "I failed," he said to Elenna.

"It seems like Kensa and Sanpao are old friends," his friend replied. "We couldn't have known that."

Tom turned at the sound of a moan. King Hugo and Aduro stood on the castle steps, their faces creased and grim.

"What a dreadful turn of events," Aduro muttered.

Tom's knees went weak. He sank to the steps, and rested his aching head in his hands. *I'm to blame for this disaster*, he thought. *Maybe Kensa was right and I'm too young to be Master of the Beasts.*

"At least we saved Henkrall," Elenna said. She rested a reassuring hand on his shoulder. "And with Kensa here in Avantia, we have a better chance of defeating her."

"Whilst she's joined forces with Sanpao?" Tom shook his head. "Combined, they might be too much for us."

"You did your best," said Aduro.

"Yes, you've served Avantia

bravely," added the King.

Tom heard a sound like parchment tearing. He spun around. Everyone – the King, Aduro, and all the guards, were looking to the centre of the courtyard where a cloud of purple smoke hung in the air. What now? Was fresh trouble brewing already? Tom scrambled to his feet, his hand on his sword. A young man appeared in the smoke, wearing a wizard's green silken robe and carrying a wand bristling with lethal spikes.

"I demand that Aduro be brought to me!" he said, drawing himself up to his full height.

The guards shuffled their feet, looking nervously from the stranger to King Hugo. Aduro waved the guards away.

"Don't worry, I don't need

accompanying," he said, stepping
forward. Tom noticed the wizard's
whole body was trembling.

"I am the Lawkeeper of the Circle of
Wizards," said the stranger. "Aduro,
you are charged with a terrible crime."

"I know this," Aduro mumbled, hanging his head in shame. "There was no other way."

"What crime?" asked Tom, standing between the stranger and the wizard.

The stranger twitched the spiked wand and Tom flew backwards into a wall and sank against the stone, winded. It felt like a horse had kicked him in the chest.

"How dare you meddle, boy!" said the stranger. "Aduro stands accused of using the Lightning Path."

Tom managed to get his breath. "But he was helping us!" he gasped

"The circumstances do not matter," said the young wizard. "Aduro, you are under arrest. You must appear before the Circle."

No, this can't be right! Tom thought. *Not after everything Aduro has done for Avantia!*

The courtyard filled with another puff of purple smoke. When it cleared, Aduro and the law-keeper had both vanished.

"Aduro!" Tom shouted, but there was only silence. With a groan, he turned to face Elenna and King Hugo.

"This can't be happening," said Elenna. "Aduro would never hurt a fly!"

"So," the king said, his voice bleak. "Kensa and Sanpao are at large in my kingdom. Aduro has been arrested. Tom and Elenna, you are weak from your difficult journey home. The situation seems more daunting than any we have faced."

"We can't give up now," Elenna protested.

Tom turned his eyes to the pennants flying over the palace. He thought of the kingdom that he loved, with its fruitful fields and shady woods and Good Beasts.

If I turn my back on this Quest, my home will be destroyed by evil forces…

There was a sudden burst of noise from the stables. With a clatter of hooves, a black horse galloped into the courtyard. A silver wolf loped alongside, tail waving.

"Storm!" cried Tom in delight. He flung his arms around the horse's sleek neck.

"Silver!" Elenna laughed as the wolf leaped at her with a yelp of joy.

Tom and Elenna's gazes locked. "Now that we have our animals again, we can tackle any Quest," Elenna said.

Tom drew his sword with a tired arm and held it aloft. He pointed its

tip at the tiny dot of Sanpao's flying
ship, hovering near the horizon.

"Our enemies will not get away,"
he said.

A smile spread across his friend's face and the King nodded gravely.

Tom sheathed his blade, placed a foot in Storm's stirrup and swung himself into the saddle. "We will fight on!"

Join Tom in The Darkest Hour,
his next Beast Quest adventure
where he will face

SOLAK
SCOURGE OF
THE SEA

Win an exclusive
Beast Quest T-shirt and goody bag!

In every Beast Quest book the Beast Quest logo is
hidden in one of the pictures. Find the logos in books
61 to 66 and make a note of which pages they appear
on. Write the six page numbers on a postcard and
send it in to us.
Each month we will draw one winner to receive
a Beast Quest T-shirt and goody bag.

THE BEAST QUEST COMPETITION:
THE NEW AGE
Orchard Books
338 Euston Road, London NW1 3BH
Australian readers should email:
childrens.books@hachette.com.au

New Zealand readers should write to:
Beast Quest Competition
4 Whetu Place, Mairangi Bay, Auckland, NZ
or email: childrensbooks@hachette.co.nz

Only one entry per child.
Final draw: 2 September 2013

You can also enter this competition
via the Beast Quest website: www.beastquest.co.uk

Join the Quest,
Join the Tribe

www.beastquest.co.uk

Have you checked out the Beast Quest website?
It's the place to go for games, downloads, activities,
sneak previews and lots of fun!

You can read all about your favourite Beasts,
download free screensavers and desktop wallpapers
for your computer, and even challenge your friends
to a Beast Tournament.

Sign up to the newsletter at www.beastquest.co.uk
to receive exclusive extra content and the
opportunity to enter special members-only com-
petitions. We'll send you up-to-date info on all the
Beast Quest books, including the next exciting series
which features six brand-new Beasts!

Get 30% off all Beast Quest Books at www.beastquest.co.uk
Enter the code BEAST at the checkout.

1. Ferno the Fire Dragon
2. Sepron the Sea Serpent
3. Arcta the Mountain Giant
4. Tagus the Horse-Man
5. Nanook the Snow Monster
6. Epos the Flame Bird

Beast Quest:
The Golden Armour
7. Zepha the Monster Squid
8. Claw the Giant Monkey
9. Soltra the Stone Charmer
10. Vipero the Snake Man
11. Arachnid the King of Spiders
12. Trillion the Three-Headed Lion

Beast Quest:
The Dark Realm
13. Torgor the Minotaur
14. Skor the Winged Stallion
15. Narga the Sea Monster
16. Kaymon the Gorgon Hound
17. Tusk the Mighty Mammoth
18. Sting the Scorpion Man

Beast Quest:
The Amulet of Avantia
19. Nixa the Death Bringer
20. Equinus the Spirit Horse
21. Rashouk the Cave Troll
22. Luna the Moon Wolf
23. Blaze the Ice Dragon
24. Stealth the Ghost Panther

Beast Quest:
The Shade of Death
25. Krabb Master of the Sea
26. Hawkite Arrow of the Air
27. Rokk the Walking Mountain
28. Koldo the Arctic Warrior
29. Trema the Earth Lord
30. Amictus the Bug Queen

Beast Quest:
The World of Chaos
31. Komodo the Lizard King
32. Muro the Rat Monster
33. Fang the Bat Fiend
34. Murk the Swamp Man
35. Terra Curse of the Forest
36. Vespick the Wasp Queen

Beast Quest:
The Lost World
37. Convol the Cold-Blooded Brute
38. Hellion the Fiery Foe
39. Krestor the Crushing Terror
40. Madara the Midnight Warrior
41. Ellik the Lightning Horror
42. Carnivora the Winged Scavenger

Beast Quest:
The Pirate King
43. Balisk the Water Snake
44. Koron Jaws of Death
45. Hecton the Body Snatcher
46. Torno the Hurricane Dragon
47. Kronus the Clawed Menace
48. Bloodboar the Buried Doom

Beast Quest:
The Warlock's Staff
49. Ursus the Clawed Roar
50. Minos the Demon Bull
51. Koraka the Winged Assassin
52. Silver the Wild Terror
53. Spikefin the Water King
54. Torpix the Twisting Serpent

Beast Quest:
Master of the Beasts
55. Noctila the Death Owl
56. Shamani the Raging Flame
57. Lustor the Acid Dart
58. Voltrex the Two-Headed Octopus
59. Tecton the Armoured Giant
60. Doomskull the King of Fear

Special Bumper Editions
Vedra & Krimon: Twin Beasts of Avantia
Spiros the Ghost Phoenix
Arax the Soul Stealer
Kragos & Kildor: The Two-Headed Demon
Creta the Winged Terror
Mortaxe the Skeleton Warrior
Ravira, Ruler of the Underworld
Raksha the Mirror Demon
Grashkor the Beast Guard

All books priced at £4.99.
Special bumper editions priced at £5.99.

Orchard Books are available from all good bookshops, or can be ordered from our website: www.orchardbooks.co.uk, or telephone 01235 827702, or fax 01235 8227703.

Series 11: THE NEW AGE
COLLECT THEM ALL!

A new land, a deadly enemy and six new Beasts await Tom on his next adventure!

978 1 40831 841 6

978 1 40831 842 3

978 1 40831 843 0

978 1 40831 844 7

978 1 40831 845 4

978 1 40831 846 1

Series 12: THE DARKEST HOUR
Out January 2013

Meet six terrifying new Beasts!

Solak Scourge of the Sea
Kajin the Beast Catcher
Issrilla the Creeping Menace
Vigrash the Clawed Eagle
Mirka the Ice Horse
Kama the Faceless Beast

Watch out for the next Special Bumper Edition OUT MARCH 2013!

SPECIAL BUMPER EDITION!

OUT NOW!

MEET A NEW HERO OF AVANTIA

Danger stirs in the land of Avantia.

Maximus, son of Evil Wizard Malvel, has stolen the magical Golden Gauntlet. Using its power he plans to force the Good Beasts, Ferno and Epos, to fight each other to the death!

NEW ADAM BLADE SERIES

Coming soon 2013

Robobeasts battle
in this deep sea
cyber adventure.

Read on for an exclusive extract of
CEPHALOX THE CYBERSQUID!

The Merryn's Touch

The water was up to Max's knees and still rising. Soon it would reach his waist. Then his chest. Then his face.

I'm going to die down here, he thought.

He hammered on the dome with all his strength, but the plexiglass held firm.

Then he saw something pale looming through the dark water outside the submersible. A long, silvery spike. It must be the squid-creature, with one of its weird robotic attachments. Any second now it would smash the glass and finish him off...

There was a crash. The sub rocked. The silver spike thrust through the broken plexiglass. More water surged in. Then the spike withdrew and the water poured in faster. Max forced his way against the torrent to the opening. If he could just squeeze through the gap...

The pressure pushed him back. He took one last deep breath, and then the water was

over his head.

He clamped his mouth shut. He struggled forwards, feeling the pressure in his lungs build.

Something gripped his arms, but it wasn't the squid's tentacle – it was a pair of hands, pulling him through the hole. The broken plexiglass scraped his sides – and then he was through.

The monster was nowhere to be seen. In the dim underwater light, he made out the face of his rescuer. It was the Merryn girl, and next to her was a large silver swordfish.

She smiled at him.

Max couldn't smile back. He'd been saved from a metal coffin, only to swap it for a watery one. The pressure of the ocean squeezed him on every side. His lungs felt as though they were bursting.

He thrashed his limbs, rising upwards.

He looked to where he thought the surface was, but saw nothing, only endless water. His cheeks puffed with the effort to hold in air. He let some of it out slowly, but it only made him want to breathe in more.

He knew he had no chance. He was too deep, he'd never make it to the surface. Soon he'd no longer be able to hold his breath. The water would swirl into his lungs and he'd die here, at the bottom of the sea. *Just like my mother*, he thought.

The Merryn girl rose up beside him, reached out and put her hands on his neck. Warmth seemed to flow from her fingers. Then the warmth turned to pain. What was happening? It got worse and worse, until he felt as if his throat was being ripped open. Was she trying to kill him?

He struggled in panic, trying to push her off. His mouth opened and water rushed in.

———

That was it. He was going to die.

Then he realised something – the water was cool and sweet. He sucked it down into his lungs. Nothing had ever tasted so good.

He was breathing underwater!

He put his hands to his neck and found two soft, gill-like openings where the Merryn

girl had touched him. His eyes widened in astonishment.

The girl smiled.

There was something else strange. Max found he could see more clearly. The water seemed lighter and thinner. He made out the shapes of underwater plants, rock formations and shoals of fish in the distance, which had been invisible before. And he didn't feel as if the ocean was crushing him any more.

Is this what it's like to be a Merryn? he wondered.

"I'm Lia," said the girl. "And this is Spike." She patted the swordfish on the back and it nuzzled against her.

"Hi, I'm Max." He clapped his hand to his mouth in shock. He was speaking the same strange language of sighs and whistles he'd heard the girl use when he first met her –

but now it made sense, as if he was born to speak it.

"What have you done to me?"

"Saved your life," said Lia. "You're welcome, by the way."

"Oh – don't think I'm not grateful – I am. But – you've turned me into a Merryn?"

The girl laughed. "Not exactly – but I've given you some Merryn powers. You can breath underwater, speak our language, and your senses are much stronger. Come on – we need to get away from here. The Cybersquid may come back."

In one graceful movement she slipped onto Spike's back. Max clambered on behind her.

"Hold tight," Lia said. "Spike – let's go!"

Max put his arms around the Merryn's waist. He was jerked backwards as the swordfish shot off through the water, but he managed to hold on.

———

They raced above underwater forests of gently waving fronds, and hills and valleys of rock. Max saw giant crabs scuttling over the seabed. Undersea creatures loomed up – jellyfish, an octopus, a school of dolphins – but Spike nimbly swerved round them.

"Where are we going?" Max asked.

"You'll see," Lia said over her shoulder.

"I need to find my dad," Max said. The crazy things that had happened in the last few moments had driven his father from his mind. Now it all came flooding back. Was his dad gone for good? "We have to do something! That monster's got my dad – and my dogbot too!"

"It's not the squid who wants your father. It's the Professor who's *controlling* the squid. I tried to warn you back at the city – but you wouldn't listen."

"I didn't understand you then!"

"You Breathers don't try to understand –
that's your whole problem!"

"I'm trying now. What is that monster?
And who is the Professor?"

"I'll explain everything when we arrive."

"Arrive where?"

The seabed suddenly fell away. A steep
valley sloped down, leading way, way deeper
than the ocean ridge Aquora was built on.
The swordfish dived. The water grew darker.

Far below, Max saw a faint yellow glimmer.
As he watched it grew bigger and brighter,
until it became a vast undersea city of
golden-glinting rock rushing up towards
them. There were towers, spires, domes,
bridges, courtyards, squares, gardens. A city
as big as Aquora, and far more beautiful, at
the bottom of the sea.

Max gasped in amazement. The water was
dark, but the city emitted a glow of its own

– a warm phosphorescent light that spilled from the many windows. The rock sparkled. Orange, pink and scarlet corals and seashells decorated the walls in intricate patterns.

"This is – amazing!" he said.

Lia turned round and smiled at him. "It's our home,' she said. "Sumara!"

Calling all Adam Blade fans!
We need YOU!

Are you a huge fan of Beast Quest? Is Adam Blade your favourite author? Do you want to know more about his new series, Sea Quest, before anybody else IN THE WORLD?

We're looking for 100 of the most loyal Adam Blade fans to become Sea Quest Cadets.

So how do I become a Sea Quest Cadet?

Simply go to **www.seaquestbooks.co.uk** and fill in the form.

What do I get if I become a Sea Quest Cadet?

You will be one of a limited number of people to receive exclusive Sea Quest merchandise.

What do I have to do as a Sea Quest Cadet?
Take part in Sea Quest activities with your friends!

ENROL TODAY!
SEA QUEST NEEDS YOU!

Open to UK and Republic of Ireland residents only.